T0131895

WE ALL HAVE A

SUPERPOWER

Written and illustrated by
Kristina Elliot

AuthorHouse™
1663 Liberty Drive
Bloomington, IN 47403
www.authorhouse.com
Phone: 1 (800) 839-8640

ISBN: 978-1-7283-2142-4 (sc)
ISBN: 978-1-7283-2143-1 (e)
ISBN: 978-1-7283-2144-8 (hc)

Library of Congress Control Number: 2019910709

Print information available on the last page.

This book is printed on acid-free paper.

Published by AuthorHouse 08/20/2019

authorHOUSE®

Dedication

For my loving husband, Ron, who always supported and encouraged my search for my own Superpower; and to my children, Sam and Dan, whose compassion and passion for what they do make me proud every single day.

Do you know how special you are?

Have
you ever
wondered
why you
are here?

Maybe you've always felt like you were made for great things.

Or maybe, like most of us, you don't quite know where you fit in.

Well SUPERHERO, it's time to look inside and see how awesome you really are.

There is only one YOU in all the world and you were born to do amazing things!

You were put here for a very important reason.

Like the trees were made to give us fruit, and shade, and a home for the birds...

Like the honeybee was made to help grow the food we eat and the flowers we love...

You were born to make the
world a better place.

No matter how ordinary you may feel...

you are absolutely perfect for the job
you are meant to do.

You don't have to be strong, or smart, or popular...

You just have to believe there's a
SUPERPOWER inside you

How Do I Find My SUPERPOWER?

Some of us feel special right from the start.

But more often your SUPERPOWER is like buried treasure, hidden deep inside you.

Like any great explorer it's your job to discover where your SUPERPOWER is hiding.

Here's a hint:

Your SUPERPOWER is something that keeps you company even when there's no one else around.

It can make you smile even when you're having a really bad day.

Find What Makes You Happy.

If your pets make you happy, maybe your SUPERPOWER is to help animals.

If you love to read, your SUPERPOWER may be telling stories or writing books.

If you enjoy drawing or painting, maybe your SUPERPOWER is to be a great artist.

If you love telling jokes, maybe making people laugh is your SUPERPOWER.

Think of your life as a treasure map.

Follow the clues, don't give up, and it will point you to the hidden prize that is your own special SUPERPOWER.

Where do you start? Just listen to your heart. It knows what your SUPERPOWER is. And if you pay attention, it will always show you the way.

Don't Be Afraid to Be You.

If you sometimes feel like you don't fit in, you're not alone. In fact, some of our biggest heroes were once just like you.

Before they were famous, Albert Einstein, Steven Spielberg, Lady Gaga and even George Washington were all teased for being different.

But they listened to their hearts, believed in themselves and used their SUPERPOWERS to become something great.

It's OK to be different!

Even if your body isn't strong. Or you don't feel as smart as others around you.

Or you look in the mirror and don't like what you see.

Remember...

Your differences might be an important clue to help you find your own special SUPERPOWER.

If you daydream a lot and can't pay attention in school...

It may be your imagination preparing you for a great career as an actor or a storyteller.

If your curiosity gets you in trouble because you need to know how everything works...

You could be preparing to become a scientist who makes the world a better place.

If you can't sit still and always need to be moving around,

your
SUPERPOWER
may be
dancing, or
sports, and
this is just
your body
showing you
the way.

Just believe in yourself.

And always celebrate your uniqueness.

No matter how hard it gets sometimes, keep on beating your own drum,

dancing your own dance,
and following your own
dream.

Be exactly who you are and accept others as well, no matter how odd they may seem.

Because like you, they're trying to find their SUPERPOWERS too.

Remember... your SUPERPOWER is there, waiting for you to find.

And once you do, it will change your life and the lives of everyone around you.

Because when you
express your SUPERPOWER
in all its awesomeness,

IT CAN CHANGE THE WORLD!

Printed in the United States
By Bookmasters